100 Quickies

100-Word Short Stories
By Chris Spencer

Every one of the following 100 different stories is precisely 100 words long (not counting each title). This particular genre involves a creative discipline to work within the restrictions of exact word count. They require the thoughtful use of adjectives, an unrelenting quest for stronger verbs mixed with a judicious use of adverbs, creative contractions and some lenient, if not radical, punctuation (perish the thought, grammarians!).

This is dedicated to my beloved wife, Jude
And
My long-suffering editing group,
The Vicious Circle

Author's note: There are 100 words on this page.

100 Quickies
100-Word Short Stories

How to Write a 100 Word Short Story

"Hmmm," I say aloud, "100 words. Easy-peasy. I should be able to write one in twenty minutes."

Sitting on my sofa with my yellow pad and sharpened pencil, I wonder . . . maybe my pencil is *too* sharp. Maybe I should open a window, get some breeze. The room is pleasant—maybe *too* pleasant. I'll adjust the thermostat. Coffee. I need coffee for inspiration . . .and a sandwich. A liverwurst sandwich. A sandwich and aaaaaa, a real cold beer instead. I should eat in the kitchen near the TV since the Seahawks are playing. Jeeze, I'm sleepy. Maybe a short nap first.

Subway Reptile

It had been a long, hard day. Robert stood transfixed on the subway platform, eyes glazed, wishing he was home. The train squealed to a stop and he shuffled aboard searching for a vacant seat, while never looking at anyone else. The car glided off and within minutes the rhythm of the clatter, the sway of the subway sucked the consciousness from his weary mind.

Robert's sleepy head lolled over onto the six-foot crocodile seated next to him, who, setting down his NY Times crossword puzzle and removing his bifocals, gently took the dozing human's head into his enormous jaws.

Runaway Boy

And I shall run away forever, said he; as little boys will say when they clash with calls to clean their room and put away their toys; and so he packs a bit of food in a scarlet bandana slung upon a stick (as seen in picture books for boys) and marches into a nearby wood to sulk upon his mother's commands and fret her indifference to his tantrum and sniffle about her offer to help him pack, and eat his sandwich, in tears, and return contrite, two hours past forever, to clean his room in time for tea.

Girl Scout Cookies

"Hey Mister, buy some Girl Scout cookies?" she chirped, enthusiastically.

"No thanks, I bought some yesterday."

"That was yesterday. How about today?"

"I'm watching my weight."

"So buy them for a friend."

"I don't have any friends."

"Okay, donate them to a food bank."

"I'm on vacation—just passing through."

"Take some home as gifts."

"I live alone."

"Give them to a stranger."

"No, I don't have room in my luggage—jeeze, back off!"

"Listen mister, I need my commission to pay for my anger-management counselling."

She pulled a machete from her green uniform.

"I'll take five boxes."

"Only five?"

A Three-Way Understanding

"I'm nervous," he said.

"Me too," she replied. "Are you sure Rose won't mind meeting me? After all, she's been your wife for 30 years and I'm just your new girlfriend."

"It'll be alright."

Ben eased the car into the parking lot. He squeezed Janet's hand and they walked silently into the Alzheimers' home.

"Rose, dear, it's Ben—your husband. I'd like you to meet someone special."

Janet, tense, stood alongside.

Rose smiled blankly, her eyes misty in the ether of faraway memories.

"Are you someone I'm supposed to love?" Rose gently asked him.

"Yes." And he began to cry.

Man-Chairs

Fred settled into one of two overstuffed chairs under the department store's escalator while his wife shopped. Waiting passively, he dissolved into the decor until you could easily mistake him for a seated mannequin sporting a flannel shirt and corduroys.

The pretty redhead arrived abruptly, and without permission, dropped into the other chair. Fred tensed.

"Hope you don't mind. I know these seats are for men, but my husband's the clothes-horse and I'm not a shopper," she cooed.

Fred relaxed. "Not a shopper? Great! But you'll need to learn the password to sit in the man-chairs." He whispered, "It's carburetors."

Love Duet

Smashed dead in the road. A great horned owl lay mangled on the center line, one talon tenderly clutching a flattened rabbit. Saddened by this unusual spectacle, I imagined neither the rabbit nor the owl could have dodged the speeding Studebaker that mowed them down. Then I saw a note held in the owl's other talon. It read,

"We are in love. Two hereditary enemies shamed by our parents to live in secret. Their ostracism is too much to bear, so with talon to paw we commit ourselves and our passion to the hereafter."

It was signed,

"Bunny & Clyde."

Operators Are Standing By

"Honey, you gotta see this. Listen to this incredible one-time special offer for fabulous stuff," says Dolores.

Earl folds his newspaper and peers at the TV advertisement.

"We need this stuff," she continues. "And if we call now they'll *double* our order."

"How much," he grumbles.

"Only $19.95."

"Plus shipping and handling. How many installments?"

"Twenty easy payments. We have to get this stuff before anyone else does."

"But what is it?" he asks.

"*What* doesn't matter—it has a certificate of authenticity."

"BFD."

"But if we call now they'll include a Popeil Pocket Fisherman."

"Gimme the phone," he blurts.

Kissing Her Instep

She lies asleep upon our bed, my wife of many years. Our passions may have faded, but not the love we have. Full pajamas have replaced her lacy negligees of yore. She snores now and I, in aging aches, sleep in restless fits and starts. But she is my wife of many years upon our bed this warm summer night and I kneel at her foot and softly kiss her bare instep as I did in our courtship days. She wakes, and smiling, pulls me close to her.

"Come to me my husband, dear, and lie here in my arms."

Ferryboat Rush

"Please Lord, let me catch this boat."

Speeding down to the ferry, I pray everyone ahead of me has ferry passes.

"Please, please!"

The Oldsmobile in front of me stops just past the booth, then backs up three feet. Its window cranks down.

"How much?" she asks.

"$8.65."

"My purse is in the trunk. I'll get it."

"Oh, God no," I wail.

She hands the attendant money. A quarter rolls under the car.

"Sorry. I've got another under the seat." She exits again.

"No, no!" I howl, and tearfully bang my head on the steering column.

Then my airbag inflates.

Geriatric Walk

I have to point it out to her while on our morning walk. At fourteen she's blind and deaf and has a slower gait.

"Bunny!" I yell. "Right there. Smell it?"

Instinctively she assumes a hunter's crouch to search the unseen rabbit. She's dreaming she can take the varmint down. I'm dreaming I can still ski moguls or hit a homerun.

But we both know better.

She takes three steps and the rabbit vanishes. She's made the show, done her job and had some fun. She keeps trying, just as I keep my skis and baseball mitt in the attic.

Cold Feet

"She's pretty, *and* available," thinks Herman.

Herman walks home alone after leaving the singles party.

"I shoulda asked her out. I'll call her when I get home."

In his apartment, he looks at the phone.

"First I'll make a drink."

Drink in hand, he stares out the kitchen window.

"I'll call her after my drink," he mumbles and turns on the TV late news.

"She's probably still partying. I'll call after one."

At 1:30 he lifts the receiver and hesitates. *She's probably asleep. I'll call her Monday. Or Tuesday.*

Herman hangs up, goes to bed.

Someday he'll call her.

Maybe.

Mailbox

The phone rings. It's my postmaster calling.

"Our mail carrier can't find your mailbox."

"That's because some teenagers knocked it off last night," I grouse.

"Your mailbox is government property. It must be replaced according to federal regulations."

"What do you mean? I *paid* for *and* installed the box on *my* post."

"Regardless of that, because the *inside* of the box is government property, it must be reinstalled according to regulations."

Two days later my postmaster calls me again chiding me about my still unreplaced mailbox.

"On the contrary," I say. "I put your part back up as per regulation."

Titanic, 1912

Cold seawater creeps up the slanting deck. My wife and daughter plead from a life raft. I hold the rail, watching their boat drift away into the night. I desperately want to be with them, but I'm glued to this sinking ship by some uniformed officer's command, "Women and children first!"

I call to my family, soon to be widowed, orphaned, "Be strong! I must obey their order and be a man."

The Atlantic swirls around my ankles. The band plays, the stars twinkle, the ship eases into the deep ocean. The dark water rises; it is cold—deathly cold.

Yard Birds

Our local poultry farmer, Mr. Bombast has many coops and plays different radio stations in each one. He insists it gives his pullets subtle taste complexities.

"So what flavor chicken are you interested in today," asks Bombast, as I peer into his freezer case.
"I've got a special on bagpipe birds."
"I tried them—tasted like plaid."
"Ok, how about Reggae?"
"Too spicy."
"Elevator music?"
"Those tasted like chicken."
"Jazz, then."
"They tasted like lizard."
"Rush Limbaugh?"
"Un-chewable."
"Gospel?"
"Aren't they mostly dark meat?"
"Not the Elvis capons."
"Got any operatic fryers?"
"Sure, I've got Madam Butterfly broilers—they're self-basters."

Inorganic Salad

"We need a dinner salad. See what Mildred has in her garden."

"Hell no. I don't want her stuff. Let's go to Mike's garage and truck garden."

"What's wrong with Mildred's organic greens?"

"She sings Wagnernian opera to her vegetables. Makes them taste overbearing and poignant."

"But her libretto lettuce compliments Bombasts' operatic chicken."

"No it doesn't. Her stuff is wilted from interminable arias."

"But Mike's lettuce is in back of the garage where he dumps transmission fluid."

"So his produce can make your heart skip."

"Alright, but only if we stop at the Poetry bakery for some Chaucer's crullers."

Over Sixty

Holding the refrigerator door open, I gaze inside. What was I looking for? It can't be ketchup, jam or milk. There's that pork chop I meant to eat last week. Now what was I looking for? Whatever it was, would it be in here?

I close the door and try to remember. If I don't stare at the eggs, hot sauce and butter it will come to me. Instead I open the door again. Crap. What was I looking for? Not anchovy paste, not horseradish, not cheese.

"Cheese! My car keys! That's it."

Now where was I supposed to go?

Goosed

Alone in her kitchen, Bertha concentrated on frying bacon. Over the sizzle, she didn't hear Mr. Jeepers sneak up behind her.

He knew what she wanted most this special evening in May. What she wasn't expecting was a goose. It caught her off guard and rouged her cheeks like a prom-night kiss. Squealing, she dropped the spatula and spun around with her arms outstretched. The room was warm in the spring twilight, her bosom heaved in anticipation.

"Give it to me, Jeepers, you rascal."

Blushing, he cocked his head, and handed her the freshly plucked dinner goose, ready to roast.

Edgar Allen Pill

I hear alarm bells calling for my pills,
capsule pills, soft-gel pills.
What a pain it is to take them for my never-ending ills.
How they rattle, rattle, rattle
in little plastic bottles, with caps that won't release in my
trembling wizened hand,
because I've lost my reading glasses and cannot read the
labels
saying damn, damn, damn,
as I drink a prune juice smoothie
to be regular today
and I'll feel a whole lot better when I finish all my pills.
From the green ones to the red ones,
Prescriptions or generic,
my pills, pills, pills.
For my never ending ills.

Three, Four, Five; Everything Changes

"You have cancer."

The doctor's *three* words fill the room, sucking out other sounds and pounding our hearts.

The wall clock stops ticking. So does our breathing. It is a moment that changes everything, shattering our complacency, comfort and immortality.

"Will it kill me?" asks my wife. I'm horrified at these *four* words. I haven't gotten to that thought yet.

The doctor looks concerned, solemn. Maybe he doesn't know *or* doesn't know how to tell us.

Holding my wife's hand, I whisper, "We will beat this thing." *Five* words I truly mean.

The wall clock starts ticking. We breathe again.

Deaf as Two Doornails

"There's a weird half-swimmer in the pool?"

Ethel rolls her eyes. "I said we're having dinner with the O'Tooles." She shouts at her husband, "Where's your hearing aid? Did you HEAR me?"

"Beer'd be great," he replies. "I'm going to my shop."

Their neighbor, Bud, calls through the screen door. "Hey Ethel, Henry home?"

"He's in the shop."

"In shock? From what?"

Ethel shouts, "SHOP!"

The men converse easily over the machinery's roar. "How's that grinder working?"

"Perfect. It grinds like a champ."

Ethel calls through the shop door. "Lunch, boys. What'd I hear about cramps?"

Henry rolls his eyes.

Requiem for a Dog

I'm done with taking walks in the cold, soaking rain. I've left behind the poop bags I always used to carry. My pockets bulge no longer with crumbling cookie bits. Gone are the staggering vet bills and scratch marks on the door. No shopping any more for the best of what she liked—no rabbit, duck or venison, no chew bones and no treats. Her fur is gone from the sofa and her food bowl put away. But I'd do it all again, oh yes, I'd do it all again for just another tail wag or lick upon my hand.

Gripe of the Magi (apologies to O. Henry)

Ethel stands grieving beside her husband's fresh gravestone. Turning, she notices a stray dog nearby, wagging its tail.

"Hello, puppy. Who do you belong to?"

Overjoyed, the dog wags harder.

"You seem so happy to see me."

"I belong to you," says the dog, licking her hand. "I'm your late husband, Herbert. I've been reincarnated as the puppy you always wanted."

Ethel's eyes widen. Gasping, she clutches her chest. Seconds later her heart stops and she keels over dead.

Instantly she reincarnates as the Corvette *he's* always wanted.

"Nuts!" he barks. "I can't drive."

So he pees on the tire.

My Turkish Hero

White bone showed below the open wound where the glass shard had sliced deeply into my skinny forearm. I was seven years old and more frightened that I'd broken the glass door than of the spewing blood. My parents away, I'd been playing tag with our houseboy, Hadji, when I crashed through the glass. Securing a tourniquet, Hadji carried me to a donkey cart he'd commandeered on a dusty Turkish road and we galloped to the village to find a seamstress to stitch me up. Looking up from the bottom of the red, bloody cart, the sky was so blue.

First Jock Strap

My first day in the locker room and coach Buford says, "All seventh grade boys need to bring a new jock strap to P.E. class on Monday."

You could have heard a pin drop.

I shudder. That means I'll have to ask Mom to buy me one. She'll want to know what size jock strap. Do I say huge? Or will she just buy a small. It'll say "tiny" on the waistband. I'll die.

"And make sure you get the right size," Buford barked.

You could have heard another pin drop. Every kid knew he was going to die.

Foreplay

There, on the 10-foot high movie screen, the glamorous temptress and the virile leading man embrace in gauzy light. Music builds as she throws her head back in surrender to his relentless grazing on her neck. Their hands search for openings and paw forbidden places. The two actors writhe, oblivious of the dark theatre's viewers.

The audience squirm in their seats, their eyes riveted in anticipation of each new thrill: the kissing, caressing, conquest, climax, cigarette. The end, credits roll, house lights go up. The agitated audience files out. Couples hold sweaty hands, race home to turn on mood music.

Teenage Pest

"Get your paws off those!" she yells. "Those are for later."

"But there's nothing to eat, Mom," he whines.

"You heard me. Go outside and get to work before dark. We need more nuts gathered."

"I don't wanna go. I have to cross the street to get more of them and you saw what happened to Chippy last week—smashed flat. It's too dangerous!"

She stops grooming her bushy tail and glares. "Spit them out. I see your cheeks are full."

Spitting out four acorns, he sulks out the knothole.

Hiding nearby, the cat watches him come down the tree.

Rust to Dust

"Harry Nourse, killed in Action, 1918."

His name plaque graces Bayview's cemetery gate.

1918—94 years ago. It's unlikely anyone alive remembers the Whidbey boy gone to war in France.

His first death came with an obliterating German bomb.

His second was a quiet ceremony to hang his plaque.

His third death is now, when no living person remembers his face, his eyes, his laugh. All that he *is* now remains in an iron plaque on an old brick gate.

Someday the final, fourth death will come. His plaque will rust away and nothing of Harry Nourse will live on.

Lost in Translation

"Can you describe, please, dis robbery?" The Italian detective, Bellini, is straining his English skills in questioning the vacationing American couple who'd just been mugged by gypsies outside the Vatican. "Wat tings was stolen?"

"My brand new Fendi handbag from the Selleria collection with Moroccan leather cross pleats, platinum Bizet latch, double-stitched Bernardo suede shoulder strap with a Fulvio deLaval buckle and Dupioni silk lining."

Overcome by her loss, the distraught wife buries her face in her hands. Detective Bellini turns to question the husband. "Wat was stolen?"

"Her purple purse," he answers.

She jerks up. "It was Venetian lilac!"

The Ties that Bind

"Who's that?" asks my teenage niece, pointing to a photo on my mantle.

"That's your grandmother—my mother. She died before you were born."

"And her?" she asks, pointing to another picture.

"Your great-grandmother, Dorothy."

She points to a third picture.

"That's your great-great grandmother, Cora, born in 1860. Cora once told me she remembered sewing with her mother the day Lincoln was shot—150+ years ago."

It saddens me that she'd never even seen their pictures before—these three special women I'd known.

"You're really old," she muses.

"As *you* will be someday," I counter.

"Not a chance!" she laughs.

Neighborhood Soothsayer

"Hey, Harold. Come in," I call to my neighbor, who's standing outside my screen door.

"Can't. Got to get these to everyone." He hands me a flyer and trots off.

I sort of know what to expect from Weird Harold, but this is special.

"Aliens have arrived from Z-2g2. They're armed with Transmogrifiers and are stealing pets. Abandon ye of all hope."

Harold's premonitions are usually about locusts or roiling skies. We'd had Cicadas once and it thundered last week, but extraterrestrials are a new twist.

Chuckling, I point the paper at my birdcage. "See this?"

The parrot is gone.

The First One Ever Eaten

Thog sits on the shoreline, holding an opened shell. Ug, dressed in rough seal skins, comes down from their tribe's cave and sits beside him.

"You catch fish?" he asks Thog.

"No. Fish spear broken. No fish. Me hungry."

"What that?" asks Ug, pointing at the slimy bivalve.

"Not know. I mad about spear. Throw this at rock. It break. Look inside."

Ug takes the shellfish and sniffs it. "Phew. What do with it?"

"Maybe eat it," replies Thog.

"No!"

"Hungry. Not eat many days. Hungry."

"No eat that. Yucky. Smelly. Gooey."

Suddenly Thog downs the oyster.

"Well?" asks Ug.

"Needs Tabasco."

Just Once, Dad

"I love you, son."

"I love you, too, Dad."

They hug, a balding black man and his son. Standing nearby in the airport waiting area, I overhear the exchange and frown. The father releases his son to the jetway and glances at me. Then anger rolls across his face.

"You disapprove? You don't think a black man can love his son?" he growls.

Startled by this unexpected outburst, I claw my way back into reality. "No," I reply. "I was actually wishing my father and I had done what you just did with your son—just once in my life."

Petty Annoyances

Leaving my car's motor running, I dash into the P.O. Okay, so I'm parked in the handicapped zone, but the place is empty. I only need two seconds to retrieve my stuff at my mailbox. A yellow package card is there.

"Must be my meds!"

I scamper to the counter but out of nowhere a woman arrives just ahead of me with three dozen boxes, all going to different countries, all having to be weighed.

Why does this always happen to me? I wonder. Twenty minutes later I sprint out the door in time to see my car towed away.

The Sunset in My Father's Eyes

My father sits in our Brooklyn apartment, looking out the window. Sunset bathes his wrinkled face in warm, orange light. Silent, he is somewhere else in his mind.

My father fought in the Pacific war and survived to see Okinawa, palm trees and coconuts. He saw Mt. Fuji, Geishas and temples. After the war, he got married and raised me and sis. Forty years he worked factory jobs to provide for us, but never left home again. He's in a wheelchair now and stares at the smokestacks and tenements, but I see the vast Pacific reflected in my father's eyes.

A Carnivore Wins a Round

"I'm a vegan!" proclaims the patron seated across from me.

I normally dine alone, but in family-style restaurants they often seat strangers together. I put my hand over my mouth in horror. "A vegetarian? Please don't say that. I'm a gardener. I love my plants. I talk to them and they talk to me. I sing opera to them. They may not be as cuddly as a chicken or a salmon, but they are alive. I can't imagine eating them. That's appalling!"

She blanches as the waiter arrives.

"I guess I'll have the veal," she quavers.

"Me too. Rare."

A Foodie's Nightmare

Her trembling body heaves with great sobs. Tears the size of Hershey's Kisses soak my *Mr. BBQ* apron. She buries her head in my armpit and I drape one arm around her while barbequing burgers sizzle on the grill. Not wishing to show divided loyalty, I furtively watch the patties with a cook's practiced eye, discretely flipping them with my spatula. I gently lay a cheese slice onto each burger. Reacting to this, she raises her head, sees the melting wedge and renews her plaintiff wail.

"No," I say consolingly, "No pretentious, imported Stilton, my sweet darling, only home-grown Velveeta."

Paris Metro

The Paris metro car pulls into the station, stopping in front of me. Through the window I see her— a serious, frumpy, middle-aged woman in a boring coat, lost in the reverie of transit travel. On impulse I smile and wave vigorously. Catching my eye, she perks up, glances sideways, and with a confused visage, tentatively waves back. The train glides down the track and I run along the platform, waving. Puzzled, she rises from her seat and waves vigorously, trying to place me in her life. The metro departs. There will be another soon. It is worth the wait.

Brand New License

Deadman's curve is approaching fast. Telephone poles are passing like a picket fence. Sixteen and just licensed, Jake and his buddies are racing his dad's powerful Packard down county road 9 in the rain.

"Go for it! You can make it!" yells Roger from the back seat.

"Take the turn on two wheels!" cries Buster.

Jake accelerates. His brakes are fair; his tires are bald.

Suddenly images from the graphic movie shown in Driver's Education flash in his mind: severed heads, broken bodies, carnage. Jake slows down. Inside his teenage brain, the pea-sized area called "common sense," doubles in size.

Bedtime Buick

Thelma was dozing in the Buick when she felt it swerve and speed up. She knew it was headed for the cliff and safely dove out the window as the car launched over the precipice. Smiling, she watched her wild-eyed husband, Louis, pass by, dragged by a rope tied to the bumper, his fingers clawing the gravel along the way.

Sitting bolt upright, Louis turned on the bed light and watched Thelma asleep beside him. Turning off the light, he was still unaware of the twine around his ankle as he warily reached for the accelerator pedal under his pillow.

Hunting the Hass

"Is this avocado ripe?" I ask the Payless produce man. "This one feels rock hard."

He shrugs. "If you want special vegetable advice, go to the Star store."

"That avocado isn't ripe," says Gene at the Star store.

"How can you tell without squeezing it?"

He blanches. "Squeeze? Never bruise a Hass' sensitive flesh. Give it here and I'll show you."

Gene holds it up to the light and turns it reverently. He sniffs the stem, then puts it to his ear and fondles the fruit.

"Hmmm. Good modular frequency," he mumbles. "Four hours in sunlight and she'll be perfect."

Chester and Molly

Deep in the whimsy-dimsy glen of Sweetbriar Wood, Chester the chipper chipmunk was singing songs of joy at the mossy edge of Bubbly Brook. Little Goober, his friend the pillow-mouse, squeaked the choruses as the two serenaded the fluttering honey-moths. Hopping through the heather, Molly, the buttery-soft, flop-eared bunny, slipped up behind them like a wisp of wind, her velvet fur radiant in the willowy sunlight, whacked Chester with a heavy shovel and stole his wallet. Opening the wallet, she found only six acorns.

"That's it? Six crummy acorns? Crap," she growled, just as Goober sliced her with a switchblade.

Deadline Pressure

Listlessly tapping the empty coffee cup on his desk, he glanced up at the newsroom clock for the fortieth time in so many minutes and knew the newspaper's deadline was intimidating itself as an ever-enlarging presence, like stogie smoke after four hours of eight ball, as he sat, unmoved but for his perspiration rising, and uninspired but for a series of amorphous and vague vignettes flitting about his brain, rummaging for an idea—a direction—for words to appear on the coffee-stained, blank paper in his typewriter and conjure up a story.

Then inspiration struck and he began to type.

Dinnertime

Dinner table manners be damned! thought Magdelena Babblejack, and she kicked her asinine brother under the table. He yelped and snorted out the chopsticks he'd stuck in his nose into the stewed chitterlings. Annoyed, Mother Babblejack lunged at her daughter with a toasting fork and missed, sinking it instead into Uncle Oofty's arm as he reached for the boiled rutabagas. Howling, he collapsed onto Aunt Snuffy, knocking her glass eyeball into the mutton chowder which scared the high-chaired baby into barfing his creamed liver and frightening the pet iguana.

Meanwhile, Father Babblejack continued grace. ". . .bless this food we are about. . ."

Seems Like Yesterday

Christmas morning and my little daughter's so giddy with excitement she's hiccupping. Wrapping paper and ribbon are floating, airborne, as she tornados through presents. The dog is prancing, my wife is giggling and grandparents are phoning us.

I jolt awake from my kitchen-table daydream on Christmas morning. My coffee's cold. My cat's asleep on the couch. I don't have a tree anymore, being a widower and too old, or lazy, to buy one. All's quiet until the phone rings. It's my daughter describing how excited my little granddaughter is with her presents. It's not the same, but it will do.

Jaded Travelers

"I don't want to go to Europe again. We always do the same things and see the same old crap."

"I'm tired of the regular stuff, too, honey. How about something different? Listen to what this travel agency brochure is selling."

"Weary of another museum? Been in one too many cathedrals? Tired of cute cobblestone villages? Waterfalls all starting to look alike? **Bob's Unique Tour Company** *offers the unexpected for the jaded traveler: witness a French guillotining, see Austria's largest hard-boiled egg, experience Monaco's sweatshops, visit Serbian abattoirs, immerse yourself in charming Spanish septic systems. "*

"Perfect! I cry. "Let's go."

Staring at Nothing

Bookends. Two old men sit, unmoving on a park bench like rusting, iron bookends. Wearing shabby coats, they each mutely stare at some fixed spot—a leaf, a twig, a penny on the pavement.

They've known one another for six decades. Fifty years ago they fought for the affections of the same pretty girl. They slandered each other's names, blackened each other's eyes. Coy and tempting, she urged them on, lured and teased them. Then in a fickle, she married someone else.

Fifty years later, they ruminate in peaceful silence, staring at nothing, unwilling to fight, even for the penny.

It's Academic

"If you know that I know, then why didn't you say you knew it?"

"Because I only said that if you *would* have known that I knew it, you might not have known *why* I knew it."

"I know that too, because she said that she knew it was well known."

"But I didn't say that she knew it too. I know that she should have known it, but because it is now something that is generally not known to those who know what it is."

"So do you know it?"

"Know what?"

"That it isn't well known."

"Next question."

Ghost on a Train

The 6:20 express train is doing 70 as it roars through the station. It passes three feet from where I'm standing, shaking the platform, howling the air. Two steps forward and I'd be a dreadful statistic; a gruesome newspaper story buried on page eight.

I board a local and find my seat—9A. Opening my newspaper, I go to page eight. There's a shocking story about some woman's bad-hair day. Then I see it, "Man struck by 6:20 express. Mister John . . ."

Before I can read further, someone sits in my seat, 9A, as if I'm not there.

Recipe Disciple

"How about I make the dessert?"

"But you don't cook," I replied. "I'm the cook in this family."

"I know, but I saw this magazine recipe for a filbert-pear tart."

"Try it," I said.

Later she griped, "Crap! I didn't buy enough pears."

"Add an apple."

"The recipe doesn't say anything about apples."

"It'll work."

"But it's a *pear* tart. And I couldn't find the filberts you said we had."

"Use hazelnuts, instead. They're the same."

"But it calls for filberts! I can't alter the recipe!"

"Improvise, dear."

"That's improper!"

"Be creative."

"OK!" And she smacked me with a spatula.

Girls Just Don't Get It

"She's coming! Get ready," Bobby whispers to Ricky.

Secreted behind a sycamore tree, the boys breathlessly await their quarry—a girl.

Ten-year old Rachel hums absently as she skips toward the trap. Both boys stick fake blood balloons in their mouths, leap from behind the tree and pretend to fight.

"Take that you miserable dog!" yells Bobby swinging his fist.

Ricky punches back simultaneously. Fake blood squirts out their lips and they both fall down, giggling uncontrollably. Rachel ignores the ketchup-stained show-offs and continues skipping along the sidewalk.

"Girls are so totally weird," says Ricky, as they watch her go.

Gangster in a Fur Coat

"So you think I can't handle it, Toots?" he growled, twirling a pistol around his crooked finger.

"It's like this, handsome, maybe you're just not big enough for the job."

"Big enough? It's an easy dog-house caper. What makes you think I can't take this mongrel out? So what's it really, sweetheart: my fur coat, the whiskers, my cheek pouches?"

She scrutinized him with her yellow eyes and took a sniff of catnip.

"Maybe you want too many acorns. Maybe your twitching, bushy tail drives me nuts. Maybe you're really just a squirrel and I'm a cat. Maybe *you're* toast."

Dead Dachshund

My neighbor stood by his garden fence holding a posthole digger and a bundle. He seemed preoccupied with a patch of ground before him as I came up the driveway. Coffee cup in hand, I leaned against the fence.

"Need to dig another posthole?" I asked, taking a sip of coffee.

"I'm just trying to remember exactly where Buttercup is buried."

I looked at the long, loaf-like bundle. My heart skipped and the coffee went cold in my mouth.

"Is it appropriate to bury a dachshund with a posthole digger?" he asked without turning, his tears dripping on his shoes.

In the Eye of the Wasp

Alone in our Turkish apartment, I answered the knock on the door. They stood there, a man and a boy, blood coating their matching aprons, knives poised, Korans held. I was seven; they were scary.

"We're here to butcher your goat," he said. "For Ramadan."

"We have no goat." I replied.

They looked disappointed. Then I looked at the son. We were the same height and he was missing an eye. Skin had grown into the socket making a little hollow in which lay a dead wasp. For a kid like me, it was way cooler than killing a goat.

Peacemaker

Shuffling noisily down the aisle, she was spoiling the peaceful serenity of the quiet cathedral. She wheezed into the pew behind me, her joints creaking audibly. Complaining about her lumbago, gout, gas and swollen glands, she desecrated the devotional silence as I prayed. I finally turned round and scowled at the irritating crone.

"Shush!" I admonished.

Ignoring me, the gorgon continued to belch and whine. Finally I'd had enough. I un-holstered my revolver and checked the bullet count.

"No, no, my son," whispered a passing priest. "Use mine. It has a silencer—won't disturb the peace. And it's been blessed."

Circular Recycling

The mountains of worthless debris my mother had accumulated over a lifetime of hoarding wasn't dwindling despite a crew of hired workers throwing the endless crap into several dumpsters. We didn't seem to be gaining on it. Mom had said that she was fine with us pitching out stuff; she knew she couldn't take it with her to the nursing home. But it wasn't until I re-discarded a familiar-looking, purple, broken typewriter that I became suspicious why we weren't gaining on the cleanup.

That midnight I caught Mom spiriting all her beloved treasures from the dumpsters back into her house.

Human Heartbreak

He leaned his trembling body over the kitchen sink and let his tears rain onto the dirty dishes. His wife was dying of cancer. It wasn't supposed to be this way; it should have been him. He looked out the window and reflected on human tragedies: of families decimated by the plague, of still-born babies and buried children, of soldiers raping, pillaging, torturing, of sailors drowned at sea. He remembered deceased parents, pets, loved ones lost forever—each one a sadness, too.

Wiping away his tears, he washed and dried the dishes and the sun shone through the kitchen window.

Trouble Brewing

Before she left for work, Jake's live-in girlfriend had hidden the coffee maker. He eventually found it behind the sink disposal but it didn't matter since she hadn't bought coffee beans and had washed the electric grinder in the dishwasher. Jake surmised she was angry about something but hadn't a clue why since her only domestic job was making coffee.

Sitting at the kitchen table with a cup of awful herbal tea, he read the note she'd left him.

"I love you."

He smiled. Then he read the rest.

"But I'm leaving you. You left the toilet seat up again."

Seven Deadly Sins: Lust

Sister Angelica slipped off her black woolen habit and wimple and slid softly into the cool lake water and out of August's heat. Minutes later, Father Hurley came through the woods to the shoreline rocks to study biblical proverbs and saw the nude nun floating on her back in the lake. Standing by her piled clothing, he closed his Bible. Only six of the seven Cardinal sins came to mind. Not gluttony, greed or sloth, not wrath, pride or envy. He couldn't remember the last one as he undressed. She'd been expecting him.

"Lust," she murmured as he dove in.

Seven Deadly Sins: Envy

"I've just got to marry Michael Jackson!" Tiffany blubbered. "Now!"

I set my newspaper down on the kitchen table and looked at my pre-teen daughter. "Why do you want to marry him? He's an odd duck," I asked.

"Dad! Pleeeeze. This is totally important."

"Why?" I pressed, against my better judgment.

"I need to show up my girlfriends."

"Show them up what?"

She rolled her eyes. "You just don't get it, do you Dad. I *need* to be the envy of my friends."

At that moment I understood what's a critical in the universe to this thirteen year-old girl.

Seven Deadly Sins: Gluttony

The prison door opened and a guard shoved in my new cellmate. Gaunt was an inadequate description. He could have been the poster boy for a concentration camp. Ribs herring-boned through his inmate's shirt. His arms were twigs and with each shallow breath his chest caved in to where I was sure I could see clear through to his spine. I motioned him to the other cot and he shuffled to it on toothpick legs, perching on the edge like a sparrow on a sill.

"I'm here for burglary. What'd they send you up for?" I asked.

He sighed. "Gluttony."

Seven Deadly Sins: Greed

Amber loved shoes. Her out-of-control obsession was aided by boyfriend, Guido, who owned a shoe factory. She loved him for his tasseled loafers, coveted him for his factory. He gave her a new pair each day. When that wasn't enough, he sold her more at cost. It still wasn't enough. Finally he left her. She wept, pleaded, obsessed, and plotted.

At Midnight, Amber broke into the factory through a skylight, accidently dropping into the massive, leather-cutting machine and hitting the start button by chance.

The night watchman pulled her out but not before she lost both legs to the knee.

Seven Deadly Sins: Pride

Elsa crept silently to the crest of the hill. Hidden in the high, tan grasses she watched the lions sprawled in the Acacia tree's shade. She was downwind—something she instinctively knew to do despite years of living with humans.

A parrot landed in a nearby bush. "What you doing, missy?" it asked the crouching lioness.

"Shush, bird. I don't know if I should go and meet them—if they will remember me or even if they are my family."

"They are your family because I remember your mother before she was killed and you abandoned. They are *your* pride."

Seven Deadly Sins: Sloth

"You're three minutes late!" snapped my boss, Frank Furious. A pencil wedged between his teeth, he didn't even look up from his twin computers while he scrawled memos and texted simultaneously.

"Sorry, chief," I whimpered. "The tsunami swept my car out to sea."

He scowled. "*I* got hit by the same giant wave and *I* still got here at five AM."

The CEO suddenly stuck her head into the office.

"I want both you slackers to work through the weekend—and no pity-party. And Frank, no more time off for your chemotherapy. I don't want sloths working in this mailroom."

Seven Deadly Sins: Wrath

Callous' iron ax neatly separated the peasant's head from its normal perch. He did this without heat or rage; it was just his job and concerned him not. A mindless mercenary, Callous focused his brutality on anyone, anywhere.

"Beware ye of my might and ax!" was his challenge.

Wrath was small and bent, but her will was strong. Callous had smote her husband and family and now he came for her. But Wrath had heat and rage and a dagger. Callous had never felt such determination as the woman drove her blade through his heart.

Wrath, a fury, was she.

Trial and Error

"Hey Dad. Come see this," my son called from the TV room.

I sat beside him and we watched a nature show about three Kenyan hunters stalking fifteen lions gorging on a wildebeest kill. The three men, armed only with their bravado and primitive spears, marched confidently into the feeding frenzy.

"Are they nuts?" I asked aloud.

The men scattered the perplexed, blood-smeared lions into the brush, hacked off a wildebeest's haunch and retreated before the confused lions could regroup.

"Well, that was way cool," my son said. "Do you suppose there was much of a learning curve for this?"

Sandpaper is for Men

"We'll get him a bouquet—pansies."

"Why flowers?" I ask my wife. "Why do people always send flowers? Jack hates flowers."

"That's what you send someone recovering in hospital."

"But he's a woodworker. Give him something he'd appreciate—maybe sandpaper."

"No. Everyone loves flowers. Nobody wants sandpaper as a present."

"I would."

"Ok. So you get him silly-old sandpaper and I'll give him a lovely bouquet."

After our visit, I heard he gave a nurse the flowers, took the sandpaper and block of wood I'd brought him, sat up in bed made sawdust, happy, for the first time in weeks.

Another New Drug

Are you one of millions of unhappy American suffering from Debilitating Chronic Nosebleed? AdNausium, a new prescription drug developed by Charlatan Pharmaceuticals, can help sufferers of DCN. Ask your doctor to order you AdNausium today and get on with your active, carefree life knowing you can stop being a heart-broken hermit due to embarrassing and deadly nosebleeds.

Take only as directed. Not for snotty infants, nursing adults, sad Asian women.

Side effects may include diarrhea, vomiting, irritable bowels, vaginal dryness, slack-jawed howling, male pattern baldness, spontaneous personal combustion, psoriasis, syntax confusion, disembowelment, flatulence and urges to become a monkey god.

Trixie's Last Chance

Trixie DuPree watched him hoist himself onto the bar stool. Even with grey hair and gigantic earlobes, he appeared younger than the other comatose patrons. He might be her last chance that night for rent money.

Trixie slid off her barstool, consciously pulling her skirt above her garter tops. He didn't notice her relocate beside him.

"Hi, big boy. Buy a lonely girl a drink?"

He turned toward the sound, fumbling with his hearing aid.

With closing time approaching, she skipped repeating her opener.

"Howbout some *super sex*?"

He squinted at her and asked, "What kind of soup is it?"

Alaska Airlines—*We're Special*

"So you're from Alaska?" I ask the fellow in Houston's airport bar.

"Ubetcha. Just come in from Anchorage on Alaska Airlines.

"Alaska Airlines—what's that like?" I query.

"It's different. Stewardesses wear snow parkas."

"Parkas? Cute!"

"Well, they have to—Eskimos prefer an unheated cabin."

"I suppose they serve walrus, too," I laugh.

"Only in first class—coach gets blubber."

"You in Houston on business?" I ask.

"Nope. I'm connecting for a flight to Fairbanks."

"But if you're going to Fairbanks, why are you in Houston?"

"All Alaska Airline flights stop here to let the ice melt off the planes."

He Loved that Tree

Wheelchair-bound, the retired sergeant sat by his city apartment window every day, enjoying a maple tree growing in a tiny square of sidewalk dirt. Each year it grew taller, cycling through the seasons. One autumn day a truck backed over the tree, killing it. Unable to replace it, the invalid mourned for his leafy friend and stared at the barren spot all winter.

In spring, another veteran from next door planted a new tree as the sergeant watched from his window. The neighbor looked up and said, "I thought you'd like a new tree, too." And they saluted each other.

Stunned Sparrow

The sparrow hits my window with a resounding thump. Outside, beneath the glass, I pick up the dazed bird and hold it in my hand. As it composes itself from the nasty wallop, I am reminded that its unexpected collision is not unlike accidents that catch *us* unprepared at times—the summersault down a staircase, the door slam on your finger, the angry yellow jackets that find you in your swim trunks. We lick our wounds, collect our wits and pull ourselves together.

The little sparrow seems fine now and, spreading ruffled wings, takes off and slams into a tree.

The Slow and Steady Fable

Back and forth the two argue. Finally the inebriated hare slams down his whiskey and challenges the box turtle, perched on the bar stool next to him, to a footrace.

"You say you can beat *me*?" slurs the hare.

"Easy-sneezy, big ears," hollers the turtle.

"Fat chance, box-boy. I'm one fast hare."

"Hare-schmare. I can whip your furry butt 'cause I'm called Turbo-Tortoise now."

"Ha! Just changing your name doesn't make you faster."

"Fifty carrots says you're toast."

"You're on, retracto-neck."

The turtle creamed the hare in a straight 50-yard dash.

Moral: *A new name can make all the difference.*

Airheads

"OhMyGod! Tiffany. Like, awesome to see you."

"Amber! Awesome! Like max to see you, too. Awesome tattoo. That, like new?"

"Yeah, like, you know, I saw in Cosmo magazine that the forehead tattoo is totally awesome now."

"Yeah, you know, like that magazine said cheek rings are totally hot and sexy too, so I had these put in."

"Awesome, but, like they look a little red and sore."

"Yeah, I think they're real infected but I got this awesome makeup to cover the puss, like, but I didn't have time to put it on this morning before my job interview."

George Gets a Licking

George, our old, cantankerous cat, didn't like it—he'd been there first. Sally, our new house pet, was ten times his weight, and a dog. But George had pet seniority and let her know it by hissing and swiping at her moist nose with his claws. She let him have his territory until the day he passed too close. Sally licked him with her enormous tongue. Not a namby-pamby, size-of-a-grape cat-tongue lick, but a soft, giant slather that lifted him off the floor.

"I guess I'll let you stay," George purred, blissfully leaning into a second lick. "Again, sweetheart, again!"

Non-Stop 8 hour Flight to Hell

Scanning the boarding airplane passengers, I'm wondering who'll be sitting next to me. Please, not the fat one—or the perfumed granny—or the garlicky talker.

A mom plops into the middle seat cradling a two-year old in her lap.

Depressed, I squeeze to the window. Hyperactive is an understatement. The little non-stop squirmer is all arms and legs.

"Now don't kick the nice man," she repeats, with no effect.

This child's lungs could compete with an air-raid siren.

Four hours later it finally dozes off just as the five-year old behind me wakes up and starts kicking my seatback.

Night of the Iguana

The iguana was slurping a bowl of beer on the Mexican bar. Lying motionless on the stained bar counter, only her tongue moved, lapping a Corona.

"What's with that?" I asked the bartender, pointing to the green lizard.

"She eat da bar's bugs. Wash zem down with cerveza."

"Is she friendly?"

"Maybe. Maybe no." The bartender shrugged.

I stared at the reptile. She and I were the only customers in the place. She stopped drinking and turned her yellow eye on me.

"Hey gringo, buy a preety girl a drink?" croaked the iguana.

Wide-eyed, I fell off my bar stool.

Fido's Obsession

Ears flapping and legs pumping, he bounds after the tennis ball I have thrown. His paws swat at the bouncing object of his fevered desire, until it's caught and subdued to his life's purpose. Proud of his grand accomplishment, he trots back with his captured treasure. Then he sees a stick in my hand. The coveted trophy that was the crux of his single-minded desire just seconds ago, drops unceremoniously from his mouth, abandoned and saliva-encrusted. His eyes rivet on the new quarry as I cock my arm to throw it. Only one of us can do this all day.

Tomb Robbers

Legendary archeologist, Dr. Mohammed Tickle, glanced over his shoulder at the setting Egyptian sun. It would be dark soon and the excavation's hired diggers would head home shortly. Apprehensive, he lingered in the shadows overlooking the sealed Pharaoh's tomb. In the moonlight, Tickle and his assistant, Sibyl Bibble, pried opened the heavy, sarcophagus lid.

"Here he lies, undisturbed for eons," exclaimed Tickle.

Their flashlights panned the shrouded mummy until the lights illuminated a papyrus-wrapped packet lying on the body.

"Dammit! Look what tomb-robbers left centuries ago!"

Sibyl opened the packet and took a bite. "Wow! These Twinkies are still edible!"

Laura Ashley Paint

I reluctantly followed my wife into the Laura Ashley boutique. Nothing had escaped the designer's signature pastel palate: clothes, croissants, butter knives, pillows, paint. Wandering the aisles, I picked up a paint can marked *"Winsome Autumn Hue—glossy/matte finish."* I showed it my wife.

"Did you see this paint? How can it be glossy *and* matte simultaneously?" I demanded.

She gave me a withering look. "It doesn't matter."

"Can *you* wear glossy and satin lipstick at the same time?" I stupidly asked.

She shrugged. "That's irrelevant. What *matters* is *her* name is on the label. Go buy us two gallons."

Pot luck Polly's Chili Con Carne

Polly was late for the potluck cooking contest. Before leaving home she strapped her hot chili entry into the booster seat and left the car door open to cool it while she rummaged the house for her raincoat.

Driving, it was sleeting hard. She squinted between the car's sweeping wipers, barely making out smeared taillights through the window. She knew she shouldn't be tailgating in icy conditions. Racing down the freeway, Polly glanced in her rearview mirror and saw two raccoons looking over her seatback, their faces smeared with chili and she slammed on the brakes. Only the chili survived.

Pirate Defense

News flash! Just into our news room.
Pirates have attacked a cruise ship off the coast of Somalia. The crew and guests of the HMS Redoubtable repelled the attackers by hurling deckchairs, mattresses, crockery and lunch meats at the pirate boats. Despite gunfire from the bandits, no one was injured, but dinner was delayed. The American destroyer Chattanouget intercepted the fleeing Somalis who swore they had just opened a beachside hotel in Mogadishu and were looking to furnish it with patio chairs, bedding, dishware and sandwiches from the cruise ship. The Navy released the pirates into their parents' custody.

Parole Board

"Have you been rehabilitated?" demands the man in the gray suit.

"Are you asking the boy I was once, or the man who's grown from that callous youth? Because I don't know where that boy is, but I know what he's become. Yes, that reckless boy killed a man and that same boy died long ago, too, like an un-watered seedling, a victim of 40 years in a prison cell. The old man before you today is guilty of nothing more than a rusted link to a child's mistake. Am I rehabilitated? You decide."

"That's no answer. Parole is denied."

Run-in with William Wordsworth

Cresting a trail on my morning hike through the dewy highlands, I come upon a tweed-caped gentleman reciting verse to the mist-shrouded moors. Not wishing to be late for my breakfast kippers, I ask him, "Pray, good sir, do you know the time?"

He pauses his poem and casts his eye upon his pocket watch.

"T'was evening erst the long-vanquished light of the night's hope wouldst

seek the breaching rays of dawn to snuff away twilight's ephemeral dusk,

and lay its bleak and melancholy mantle upon so sweet a sunrise."

"Shit. Another goddam Lake poet," I grouse.

"It's 7:35, asshole."

Gone, but not Forgotten

My wife took my arm and pointed at a family plot in a lichen-covered graveyard. "Look at this," she said, pointing at a row of bantam gravestones. "Six young children, died one by one, year after year. How does one survive such tragedy?"

A hoarse whisper came from behind us. "You get over it." She trudged past us and stopped at the family plot. Dressed in black, bent with age, she tenderly laid a fresh bouquet beneath each child's headstone.

She turned to us and spoke, her voice cracked with sorrow. "They were all mine, once . . . you get over it."

Mom's Ashes

"Scatter my remains over Paris," was my mother's deathbed request. I didn't think she was serious, since we'd always played practical jokes on each other, but she was dead earnest. So three weeks later I solemnly climbed the Eiffel Tower with a rosewood box of ashes. At the top, I opened the case and sailed the powdered scraps into the breeze.

I was fined 500 francs for littering. I'm sure Mom was looking down from heaven, smoking her eternal cigarette and gleeful that she'd one-upped me one last time.

But touché!—they weren't her cremated remains, only her cigarette ashes.

Shiloh, 1862

It only took a second for the Union Minié ball to cross the wheat field. Marching into battle, the Confederate soldier-boy saw the flash of yellow, musket fire but had no time to crouch. It only took a second—just half a rebel yell—one frightened step.

The lead slug hit his chest, splintered the keepsake daguerreotype of his mother, ripped through his heart and lodged in his spine. Death only took a second.

His comrades buried them together, his mother's fledgling boy *and* the bullet, in an unmarked grave in an unknown field in a place she'll never see.

What I, the Red Baron, Do at Home

My shot just grazes my enemy's wingtip as he revs up, rolls over and dives into a vortex spin. Anticipating his rotation, I turn, reload my weapon and strike where he should be, barely missing him again. He may be dodging madly to elude me but I know he'll end up cornered and confused when he hits the kitchen window.

"Gothcha! You varmint," I yell, as my rolled-up newspaper smunches the horsefly on the glass. My adrenaline surging with the relish of the domestic dog-fight, I hear another fly buzzing nearby, raise my swatter and adjust my aviator goggles.

Bad to Worse

Sprinting across the midnight moor, Jocko didn't see the badger hole. One leg plunged downward, stopping at his crotch. Sharp stones ripped his flesh. Momentum scattered his stolen silverware into the heather. The hole held him fast. A shooting pain gasped him—he knew his bowels were bleeding. Close by, hounds bayed, lanterns danced and voices shouted.

"Damn!" he hissed through clenched teeth. "This was stupid. I'll not go to prison again! Nothing could be worse than that!"

In the hole below him the hungry badger tasted dripping blood, bared its razor teeth and lunged upward to Jocko's bleeding bowels.

Stone-Deaf Prophet

"Have ye questions ye wish to ask?" inquired the prophet.

"O wise one, tell me about the Old Testament."

"Drafty it was. And the plumbing didst leak. A six-floor walk-up with no elevator. Landlord from hell. Philistines for neighbors. Burn they their goats in the corridors and eat hummus with their left hands. Come Sabbath did they swill mead and gossip like drunken harlots at the well."

"What's that got to do with the Old Testament?"

"Oh, I thought you asked me about the *old tenement* where I used to live?

"No, but I wanted to know about that, too."

Irish Peasant's Lament

Erin's second miscarriage devastated her far beyond what she'd thought possible. Curled fetally in her horsehair bed, she neglected her household, wasting days in a torpid haze.

"We must try again, lass," pronounced her crofter husband. "We need children to harvest potatoes, carry water, do chores."

"No," she sobbed.

"We must."

"Never. It hurts too much."

"The pain will pass."

"Not in my heart."

"'Tis God's will."

"To suffer this much?"

"No. To keep trying," he urged, leaning down. "Besides, third time's the charm."

Erin uncurled, rolled upon her back and took her husband in.

"For God, then," she sighed.

Mom's Battered Chicken Recipe

Having chicken for our Sunday supper meant first catching a nimble bird. Our Mom had a great technique for doing this. She'd bait an old, back-porch washing machine with cracked corn and leave its door open. When a chicken followed the trail in, she'd slam the door shut and set the machine to heavy-wash. After the spin cycle she'd easily catch the stunned, de-feathered bird as it staggered out. Pulling a stiletto from her garter-belt, she'd decapitate on the spot and cook the fowl for dinner.

Sadly, all our roast chickens looked like they'd been bruised in a laundromat brawl.

College Days

Turning his grizzled head slowly on the pillow, he focused on the university campus, framed in the hospice room's window—his last room—his final view.

For 60 years he'd tied his life and destiny to this university as a student, professor, dean and finally provost. His wife, children, colleagues, were now just bones in his alma mater's body, made of ivy and traditions. Numberless life events fused together in this collegiate oasis—his oyster.

As he closed his eyes, all he could remember was his plea, made 60-odd years ago, "Please, coach, let me carry the football just once."

The Seer and the Penitent

The seer patted my heaving shoulder. "I see you weep, feel your anguish. You have lost love and are searching to know why your aching heart constricts."

"I *am* suffering," I cried.

"Billions of tragedies have preceded yours, countless more will come. Unending sorrow has been drowned in oceans of tears since mankind first learned to grieve."

"Will my pain pass?"

"Balance agony and pain with equal amounts of joy and peace and you'll have all human history."

"But *do* they ever balance out?" I pleaded.

"That depends on whether your cup is half full or half empty, my son."

Mystery Teaser

Prudence quietly turned the latchkey and eased the front door open. She hesitated, listening for any sound before tiptoeing into the moonlit kitchen. From her purple handbag she pulled out a jar of paper wasps, one pink glove, a broken pocket watch and a mother-of-pearl penknife and put them on the counter. A loud snore erupted from a nearby room. Startled, she froze, waiting until the sleeper found his rhythm. Pocketing a ripe peach and a percolator, she popped open the wasp jar and dashed outside.

She relocked the door and hissed, "Figure that one out, you dumb palooka."

Hooked With a Pickle

"Exactly what *are* you going to do with that dill pickle, Phyllis?"

Roger's wife, Debbie, looks around the kitchen, empty but for the two of them. "What the hell does that mean?" she demands. "What pickle? Who's Phyllis?"

He grins. "It's the first line of my next novel— it's the hook."

"It won't work," she quips. "Nobody cares about some goddam gherkin."

After stewing for a minute, Debbie asks, "So what about Phyllis' pickle? Is it some kind of weapon— a covert quest—a romantic secret—smut? Well?"

"Good. You're hooked," he said, beaming. "Buy the book."

"Discount price?"

"Maybe."

Going Over

He went to the train station to join his wife. He hadn't seen her in three years and missed her terribly. The train would take him to her. And she would be waiting for him—*over there*.

Stepping onto the platform's yellow, warning edge, he watched the approaching engine hurtle toward him. The twin steel rails gleamed below. He was dying to see her.

He timed his last step into the void before him, plunging down as the locomotive arrived. But the instant before the engine struck, a final thought crashed into his mind; what if she wasn't—*over there?*

Prenuptial Negotiations, Arab style

"We need to clarify this agreement. I want six dogs."

"Two dogs, maximum."

"Four dogs and three cats."

"Three cats and my parrot."

"I hate that parrot."

"You're breaking my heart. If it goes I want a turtle and a snake."

"No snakes. Maybe a turtle. Three dogs, one cat and my hamster, final offer."

"You're ruining me. Ok, two dogs, two cats, and a turtle."

"Done."

"Let's get married."

"Ok, but I want six bridesmaids."

"Two attendants, max."

"Four, three flower girls, in a church."

"A best man, matron of honor and a justice of the peace."

"Done."

"Honeymoon?"

Convent Combat

"Heathens have breached the convent's walls!" bellowed Mother Superior, strapping on a Smith & Wesson semi-automatic and her combat crucifix. "We can't let them reach the vestry. They'll ravage the..." Her voice trailed off as she charged out the door.

Sister Mary looked horrified, crying, "Ravage the what? Not. . . the novices! Wait for me!"

But Mother Superior, her habit flapping, was already charging down the hall in sensible shoes. Sister Mary grabbed the nunnery's tommy gun and followed, cocking it as she ran.

"No, not the novices," Mother S. yelled back over her shoulder. "The pagans want our sacramental wine!"

House of Cards

"That's an impressive house of cards you've built," said the raven to the old man sitting at the table.

"It's taken me 83 years to construct this," he wearily responded. "Slow and steady—one card at a time.

A knock at the door turned both their heads.

"Time's up," cawed the bird.

The door burst open. A wind gust dismantled the man's 83 years of work and bore him out the door and left a newborn lying on the table. The door slammed shut.

The raven gathered the cards and placed the deck before the infant.

"Your turn. Start building."

Made in the USA
Middletown, DE
09 July 2024

56791170R00057